Contents

1

The Grey Stranger

The orphans stood in two silent rows in the hall, girls on one side, boys on the other. Mr Portly was expecting someone. Someone who seemed to make him nervous. He moved slowly as if he were at the head of a great procession but there was only Mrs Warming scuttling behind him. He stopped by the tallest boy.

"Are you working hard, Jebediah Smith?"

"Yes, sir," said Jeb. "Very hard, sir."

"As hard as you, sir," murmured young Sam.

"Silence!" roared Mr Portly. "Who asked your opinion, Samuel Hardacre?"

A little snorting sound came from the girls' row and Mr Portly swung round.

"Did I hear a snigger? Was that you, Lizzie Andrews?"

Meg, the eldest girl, frowned at her, trying to make her behave. Lizzie bobbed politely and smiled sweetly. "Me, sir?"

Mr Portly glared at her. "If you know what's good for you, you will keep silent." He prowled along the line a little further. "Things have become very slack of late, Mrs Warming. More strictness is needed."

"Oh, *yes*, sir," said Mrs Warming.

Mr Portly smiled unpleasantly. "Things will change when s*he* comes, I assure you."

"Look at these children," he continued, "are they not well dressed?" He hardly bothered to look at the children in their old, worn clothes. "They may be orphans but they have the best of everything."

"They do work hard for it," ventured Mrs Warming.

"Hard? Hard? They should think themselves lucky to work for Portly's Superior Sweets. They should be proud. Without my genius, they would be sleeping in doorways."

Now, this was not quite true. It was true that without the orphanage the children would have been sleeping in doorways but it was not true that Mr Portly was a genius.

Mr Portly's business was making sweets. Mrs Warming was supposed to be in charge and, although she was a wonderful cook, she did not have any imagination. The children had the imagination. Every year, they won first prize at the town's Festival which was very important to Mr Portly's business. They were the geniuses. Mr Portly had nothing, really, except money and a good opinion of himself.

Mr Portly finished his inspection and went to stand by the front door. He took a large, round watch from his waistcoat pocket, glanced at it, then swung the chain.

"It is a few moments to eleven. At eleven o'clock, I expect your new mistress to arrive. Mrs Warming will still be in charge of the sweet making, of course, but at all other times, your mistress will command you. You will address her as 'ma'am' and speak only when spoken to."

Just then, the

hall clock began to strike. At the same moment, they heard a coach rumble into the cobbled yard. Mr Portly nodded in satisfaction and put his watch away.

Meg, the eldest girl, went towards the door but, before she reached it, it swung noiselessly open. Even Mr Portly jumped.

In the doorway stood a tall, thin shape, dressed entirely in grey. A long, grey dress matched a grey bonnet. Even her face was grey except for pale, yellow eyes.

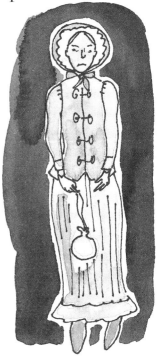

As she moved, she seemed to glide, like a ghost.

The coachman appeared behind her, carrying a black trunk. He seemed uneasy. The woman opened a grey cloth bag. She found some coins and held them out to the coachman. He took them and bolted out of the door. As he ran down the steps, they could see him wiping his hand on his coat.

Meg shut the door. The noise seemed to revive Mr Portly. "Well, well," he said. He held out his hand but the woman did not take it. Instead, she turned her yellow eyes on the children. Mr Portly coughed.

"These are the orphans," he said. He coughed again. "This is your new mistress, Miss Cold."

2

Miss Cold

Miss Cold began her duties that night. Even Mrs Warming was quiet as she ladled the gruel and cut up large hunks of the fresh bread that the orphans themselves had made. Miss Cold stood in the doorway, a grey statue. She said nothing until Mrs Warming brought more bread.

"Mrs Warming!"

"Yes, ma'am?"

"Is that extra bread?"

"Yes, ma'am."

"Take it away."

"But ma'am, it's just bread!"

"They will learn to be greedy. They have already had half a bowl of gruel and a piece of bread. Is that not enough?"

They all stared down the room. With the dark hall behind her, Miss Cold's figure was very dim in the doorway. All they could see clearly were the yellow eyes.

"The meal is over," said Miss Cold. "Go to your beds. I am coming to inspect them."

Then she was gone.

"She's horrible!" hissed Lizzie.

"Shh!" whispered Meg. "She'll hear you."

They scampered up the back stairs

but there was not much to tidy. Each bed had a thin mattress, a blanket and a hard pillow. They washed under the pump in the yard. There was just one big cupboard in each room where the Sunday coats and bonnets and caps were kept. They wore them for church because there, people could see them, and would think Mr Portly looked after them well.

They could hear Mrs Warming puffing and panting up the stairs. They didn't hear Miss Cold as she glided up and into the girls' bedroom.

She walked slowly between the iron bedsteads. "Good," she murmured. "We do not need elaborate furniture. What's this?" she continued, stopping abruptly by the youngest girl's bed.

"What do you mean, ma'am?" whispered Sally.

"*Two* blankets? What ridiculous luxury."

"It's because of Sally's cough," said Lizzie boldly. "She mustn't get cold."

"What nonsense," Miss Cold said smoothly. "She must not imagine she is delicate. Take it away."

Mrs Warming opened her mouth, then shut it again.

Miss Cold stopped by an empty bed. "What is this?"

"That's for the new girl, ma'am. Coming tomorrow. There's a boy, too. Brother and sister."

"I will inspect the boys' dormitory now." Miss Cold left as silently as she had come and the girls remained absolutely still until they heard Mrs Warming wheezing and creaking down the stairs behind her new mistress.

"Well!" exploded Lizzie, as they all came out on to the landing. "I could kill her!"

"What shall we do?" asked Meg anxiously, hugging Sally to her.

"I'm going to see what I can find out from Mrs Warming about the Festival," said Lizzie. "Don't forget, if

Old Portly is going to win, he needs us. Miss Cold can't change that."

She returned with her arms full. "Mrs Warming is definitely on our side," she announced. "She doesn't like Miss Cold one little bit. She's sent Sally's blanket back and she says we might as well have this."

She passed round a large basket of fresh, crusty bread.

"It's got butter on it!" gasped Sam.

Lizzie grinned. "Mrs Warming says Mr Portly has set his heart on winning the Gold Cup at the Festival. If we have some brilliant ideas, he won't care about anything else. We'd better get thinking."

"Yes," said Jeb, slowly. "I might be getting an idea. Let's sleep on it."

"Don't be frightened," said Meg. "Together we can beat Miss Cold. I'm sure we can!"

3

The Newcomers

Meg was carrying a heavy tray. Under silver lids lay rashers of bacon, steaming heaps of mushrooms and golden eggs. There was a delicious smell of coffee escaping from the tall coffee pot. She thought miserably of the orphans' bread and water breakfast.

She knocked at the big oak door.

"Come," called Mr Portly.

He and Miss Cold were seated at opposite ends of the table. Standing just inside the door was a tall, thin girl with long, black hair, holding a little boy by one hand and a leather bag in the other.

"Ah, Meg," said Mr Portly, starting on the bacon, "here are the new orphans."

Miss Cold interrupted him. "Take them away, girl. Set them to work."

As the door was closing, Miss Cold spoke again. "The boy is too small to work. He will have to go."

In the kitchen, the children were stirring pots of chocolate when Meg burst in. Her face was red with indignation.

"This is Hannah and Tim and SHE wants to turn Tim out already!" They knew whom she meant.

"We won't be separated," said Hannah. "We'll run away now!"

"But how will you live, dear?" asked Mrs Warming.

"I'll draw pictures and sell them in the street."

Meg gave her a comforting hug.

"*Can* you draw?" Lizzie put a piece of paper in front of her. "If you can, that may help. This is Jeb's new idea."

"The best yet," beamed Mrs Warming. "We'll win the competition with these chocolate boxes."

"But everyone does boxes of chocolates," objected Meg.

"Not like these," explained Lizzie. "These boxes are *made* of chocolate. Then, you see, they can be decorated and filled in all sorts of ways."

Hannah was enchanted. "I could help with that." She quickly sketched a design for a toy box.

"Perfect!" exclaimed Meg. "Try some more ideas."

As they worked, Lizzie asked Hannah about her family.

"I don't know where they are now." Hannah swallowed. "We were all sailing home from India and there was a terrible storm. I just remember the dark and the bangs and screams. Before we were separated…" Hannah stopped, then went on, bravely, "Mother tied this bag round my waist. She made me promise two things. One was to look after Tim, the other was to keep this little medal with a picture of a ship on it. She said something strange," continued Hannah. "She said, 'Don't ever lose the little ship. It may sail you home.'"

The other children stared at the medal. They had never owned anything and could not remember their parents. Then they heard a loud voice outside the kitchen door and Mr Portly bustled in. Miss Cold glided in behind him.

"Now, my dear," Mr Portly said to Hannah, "I've found an excellent place for your little brother. Mr Sawyer needs a sweep's boy."

"We must stay together." Hannah spoke in a low but firm voice. Mr Portly looked taken aback.

"No matter," said Miss Cold. "She can go, too. She does not look strong."

"Hannah's been helping us, sir," said Jeb, loudly. "See these boxes? We've done you a little example."

Mr Portly immediately turned all his attention to the chocolate boxes. "What a novelty!" he chortled. "Quite original! No one has ever done anything quite like that before."

"This is a toy box. See all the little toys? Hannah did that." Jeb took the paper that she and Lizzie had been working on and waved it under Mr Portly's nose. "Lovely, isn't it? I don't think we want to lose Hannah."

Miss Cold drummed her fingers on the table. Her voice was quiet when she spoke. "Who are these children, Mr Portly?"

"Poor little homeless waifs and strays, Miss Cold. It is fortunate for them that I am so charitable."

"What is your name, girl?" Miss Cold examined Hannah through half-closed eyes.

"Hannah Fitzgerald, ma'am."

"And is that all you own?" She pointed to the bag.

"Yes, ma'am."

Miss Cold's pale, bony wrist flashed as she stretched out her hand. Hannah watched in alarm as Miss Cold opened the bag.

Mr Portly was clucking round the chocolate sample so he did not see her unrolling a large, official-looking document.

She rolled it up carefully and when she looked up again, her yellow eyes were hooded. She had a faint smile on her lips.

"I will take care of this bag," she said, quietly. Then she announced, "Of course they must stay, my dear Mr Portly."

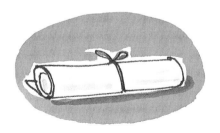

4

The Plan

Hannah was very upset about her bag.
Although Tim was too young to
understand what had happened,
Hannah's unhappiness frightened him
and he started to cry. Sally and Sam sat
on the kitchen floor with him and fed
him tiny pieces of chocolate.

Hannah was almost crying, too.
"It's all I have left. They were my
family letters. Then there was that big
document. I couldn't read it," she

confessed, "the words were too hard. It had a big, red seal on the bottom. Then there was that silver medal I showed you – the ship on it was a picture of my grandfather's ship, the *Silver Dolphin*."

"So anyone from your family would recognize it," said Jeb, thoughtfully.

"Miss Cold seemed very interested

in that document," interrupted Lizzie. "Did you notice? She was all ready to send Tim and Hannah away until she looked in the bag. I'm going to her room tonight to get it back."

"Oh! Lizzie!" gasped Meg. "You mustn't! She'll catch you and then you'll get turned out!"

"I don't care," said Lizzie. "She's not going to get away with it."

"Then I'll come with you," said Hannah.

"You're mad," said Jeb. "You can't do it!" The girls said nothing. He hesitated. "But if you're going, then I'd better come, too."

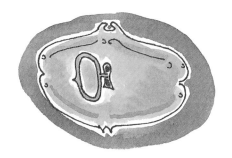

5

In the Dark

All three stood outside Miss Cold's
room in the darkness, hardly breathing.
Lizzie peeped through the keyhole.
Very quietly, she turned the door knob.

The room was quite dark. Only a
sliver of moonlight fell across the desk.
Across Hannah's bag.

On one side of the room was the
huge, four-poster bed. The bed curtains
were closed so Lizzie made a daring

decision. She set off across the room, moving noiselessly. Reaching the bag, she lifted it gently. She started back towards the door. She did not notice the little footstool until she stumbled over it. They stood utterly still, almost unable to breathe.

Nothing happened.

Lizzie paused by the bed, listening carefully. Then, to Hannah's horror, she pulled back the bed curtains.

"She's not here!"

"Then let's get out while we can," whispered Jeb.

Hannah took her bag and scrabbled in it.

"The letters and the medal are here. The big paper is missing."

"For goodness sake!" Jeb's voice was urgent. "Let's go!"

As they crossed the hall, they saw a

light. It moved and swayed. Someone was in the kitchen, carrying a candle.

They slipped silently into the shadow of a doorway. They saw a candle, held high, moving across the room, throwing flickering shadows on the wall. In the darkness, the candle seemed to be travelling alone.

"It's Miss Cold," whispered Jeb. "I think she's about to go out."

They stood in the dark until they heard the kitchen door open. The candle was put down and flickered in the draught. They heard Miss Cold go down the back steps.

"Lizzie! Come back!" gasped Jeb but Lizzie had already crossed the kitchen and was listening at the door. She could not see but she could hear.

"So you have come," said Miss Cold.

There was a rustle. "This is the document. The will leaves everything, money and property, to the two children. It should be a simple matter to make me their guardian."

"Maybe, but only if they have no family." A deeper voice. A man's.

Miss Cold's voice cut in, quiet and venomous.

"According to that fool, Portly, the parents were drowned at sea. The children are probably thought to be dead, too. By the time they are discovered, if ever, I shall be far away with the money."

"Give me the document and I'll see what I can do."

There was another rustle as the paper changed hands. Lizzie had heard enough. Softly, she closed the door and turned the key in the lock.

"Dear, dear," she said, "I do believe Miss Cold has been locked out."

In the attic, Meg was very glad to see them back.

"So that's what that paper is for!" Jeb said. "It's to say who gets all your parents' money, Hannah. Miss Cold is going to arrange things so she gets it instead of you and Tim."

"You must find your relatives," said Meg, anxiously. "Those letters must have been from someone. Aren't there any clues?"

"The only other thing I have is the *Silver Dolphin*."

"I wonder what your ma meant," Lizzie wondered, "when she said, 'It may sail you home'?"

Hannah shook her head sadly and Meg gave her a hug.

"It's a lovely ship, anyway. I'd

like to draw it."

Jeb gave a sudden little yelp. "That's it! That's what we'll do!" He grinned at their surprise. "We'll make chocolate treasure chests, filled with exact copies of the *Silver Dolphin* medal. Soon, everyone will see Hannah's *Silver Dolphin*!"

6

The Grey Guardian

The next morning, Mrs Warming bustled cheerily about. "Miss Cold is staying in bed today."

"Something serious, I hope," murmured Sam.

"She has a chill. I found her on the doorstep this morning, wet through. She says she went out for an early stroll and was caught in the rain."

"Fancy that," said Lizzie calmly.

"'Don't think of coming out of your room today, Miss Cold,' I said. She did look terrible, I must say."

"She always does," said Sam. They set to work, feeling as if a huge, dark cloud had been lifted.

They were all grouped around the table, Sally standing on a box. Even little Tim was helping Sam to stir the chocolate.

When he came to inspect the

finished boxes, Mr Portly was delighted. "Splendid!" he said. "Portly's Superior Sweets is going to triumph once more. The ship is an excellent touch, just right for a seaside town like ours. I shall draw the Mayor's attention to it. Mrs Warming, the children may have butter on their bread at supper."

"Very well, sir," said Mrs Warming. "And if you win, perhaps we could have a cake?"

"Cake? Cake? Have you taken leave of your senses? Children such as these could not digest cake. In fact, perhaps they had better not have the butter. Tomorrow, Jeb, be ready at seven o'clock sharp to set up our stall at the Festival Hall."

The next morning, Jeb loaded his handcart and set off.

"It's the best ever," beamed Mrs Warming as they settled down to wait.

In the middle of the afternoon, however, Mr Portly returned unexpectedly, followed by Jeb.

"Mr Portly, sir!" said Mrs Warming. "Didn't they like it?"

"Yes, yes, a triumph," said Mr Portly, absently, "but something quite extraordinary has happened. My most important customer came in, with his wife. He was delighted and we started to do business but his wife became as pale as death, staring at the ship design."

Behind Mr Portly, Jeb was pulling the most peculiar faces and pointing to Hannah and Tim.

"I explained that these children designed the ship and they are coming here, at once. It makes no sense. The woman was almost hysterical. Anyway, he is an important man, Mrs Warming, so we must prepare to make them very welcome. Come along."

Jeb was nearly bursting. "I'm sure the lady recognized the *Silver Dolphin*. We must make sure they meet Hannah and Tim."

He was interrupted by Mrs Warming who hurried back into the kitchen, looking puzzled. "They've all gone mad today," she complained. "Hannah, Tim, Miss Cold wants you. You've to go to the morning room immediately."

"What's happening?" asked Lizzie. "I'm going, too." They all followed.

As they entered, Miss Cold rose to her feet, smiling her wolfish smile. Her gloves were on the table and her travelling bag was ready by the door. On the table lay Hannah's precious document. Sitting beside Miss Cold was a man. Lizzie suddenly felt afraid. Miss Cold turned to Hannah and Tim.

"This is a very happy day," she said. "We only have to sign this and then, my dear children, you will belong entirely to me. I am to be your new guardian." She smiled again. "We are going on a train journey. We leave at once."

7

Too Late?

"Come quickly, sir," shouted Lizzie.
"Miss Cold is taking Hannah and Tim
away."

Mr Portly had been choosing wine
in the cellar. He puffed up the steps
and hurried to the front door.

It was too late. All they saw was the
back of the carriage as it turned the
corner. Mrs Warming cried and Mr
Portly shouted. Only Jeb and Lizzie
kept their heads.

"They are going to the station," said Jeb. "Lizzie, we'll follow them. When the strangers come, Meg, tell them everything."

The station was full of people and full of noise.

They ran up the steps of

the bridge and looked down on the
crowds. The trains blew clouds of
steam.

Then Lizzie saw them. "Look, look!"

she shouted. "At the ticket barrier!"
Miss Cold was dragging Tim and
Hannah towards the barrier. A train
was already waiting at the platform
but there was a queue.

"I'm going to get them." Jeb was
already clanging down the iron steps.

One by one, the passengers were going through. Now, there was only one person in front of Miss Cold and the frightened children.

She was a stout, jolly woman and she was having some difficulty with her enormous travelling bag.

"You'll have to lift it over, madam," said the ticket collector. He winked. "Can't get you both through at once."

"Move aside, instantly. I must get that train." It was Miss Cold. She pushed Tim forward so roughly that he banged his face on the barrier.

"All in good time," said the ticket

collector. "Be careful of the child."

The stout woman dropped her umbrella. A little boy, holding a stick of bright pink candyfloss, ran forward and picked up the umbrella. He stood enjoying the drama.

"I insist that you let me through."

"I'm waiting for this lady's ticket," said the man. He did not like Miss Cold.

"I've got it in my bag. I know I have." The poor woman was flustered now. All sorts of things started to fall out of the bag. People helped to pick up rolling oranges, knitting needles and mysterious and vast items of clothing.

"My good woman." Miss Cold began to lose her icy control. Her voice became shrill, "You are stupid and ill-organized. Stand aside."

"Don't you 'good woman' me!" shouted the stout lady, turning on her.

"I've had just about enough of you! If you're so clever, you find it," and she thrust her bag at Miss Cold.

Miss Cold stepped back, sharply, right into the candyfloss.

"Ooh!" squealed the little boy, "you've got a pink, fluffy tail, just like my bunny."

Hannah moved. She grabbed Tim and ran.

"Over here!" yelled Lizzie.

But someone else was shouting, too. "Hannah! Tim!"

Jeb saw the two strangers who were running towards them, with Mr Portly panting behind.

The woman threw her arms around Hannah and Tim. "The moment I saw our ship, the *Silver Dolphin*," she cried, "I knew we had found you at last!"

Although it was only Saturday, all the orphans were in their Sunday clothes.

They were somewhere they had never been before – in a teashop. Sally was staring at everything in wonder, Sam had cake in each hand and Lizzie was licking her fingers. Meg just smiled and smiled.

Hannah and Tim's aunt, holding

Tim on her knee, praised them over and over again. "You were so clever!" she said. "We shall never be able to thank you enough."

"The *Silver Dolphin* did sail us home." Hannah took the medal out and looked at it.

"Your aunt recognized it at once," said their uncle. "Well done, Jeb. I understand that was your idea. For the moment, however, can we reward you with another cake? Chocolate? Cream? What would you like?"

"What I'd really like," grinned Sam, scattering crumbs from his seventh cake, "is to have seen Miss Cold's face when she got that candyfloss tail!"

"You would, Sam," sighed Meg. "You would."

About the author

Victorian readers liked a good melodrama. That's a story where everyone is either very wicked or very good. A bit over the top. So it seemed a good idea to write this story in a Victorian way. Miss Cold is wickedly cold-hearted, Mrs Warming is warm-hearted and Mr Portly is a pompous ass. The orphans, although they are treated as orphans were in those days, are the heroes. They are resourceful and kind to each other, although they have nothing.

I suggest you feel free to cheer and boo the different characters as the audience would in a Victorian theatre!